Depression Recovery Roadmap

Overcoming Depression

Deepak Singh

pencil

ISBN 978-93-5667-743-2

Published in India 2023 by Pencil

A brand of
One Point Six Technologies Pvt. Ltd.
Unit no. 26, Ground Floor, Building A1,
Wadala Truck Terminal Road,
Near Post Office, Antop Hill, Mumbai - 400037
E connect@thepencilapp.com
W www.thepencilapp.com

DISCLAIMER: *The opinions expressed in this book are those of the authors and do not purport to reflect the views of the Publisher.*

Author biography

Hello! I'm happy to meet you, I'm Deepak Singh. I work as a research analyst and am passionate about writing books and doing research on the planet Earth, space, and the art of living. I most likely have high analytical and critical thinking abilities that enable me to assess data, spot trends, and reach conclusions in my capacity as a research analyst. As part of my job, I might perform primary and secondary research, analyze available data, and provide findings to guide individual, corporate, or organizational decision-making. I adore writing and researching as interests in space and Earth in my free time. You can tell that I have an open mind and am interested in learning about the world around me.

CONTENTS

Foreword

Depression is a frequent and serious mental health problem that affects millions of people around the world. While the stigma associated with mental health has lessened in recent years, many people continue to struggle to find the help and support they require to recover from depression. This is why the book "Depression Recovery Roadmap" is so vital.

The writers of this book have chosen a compassionate and evidence-based approach to tackling depression, providing a complete guide to recovery that covers everything from depression's causes and symptoms to evidence-based therapies, coping skills, and creating a support network.

As a mental health professional, I've witnessed firsthand the devastation that depression can cause for individuals and their loved ones. This book provides a practical and powerful road map to recovery that can assist individuals in regaining control of their mental health and living fulfilling lives.

The authors have done an outstanding job of simplifying complex concepts and offering real examples that readers can connect to. The book is written with care and understanding, offering hope and direction to those suffering from depression and their loved ones.

I strongly suggest "Depression Recovery Roadmap" to anyone wishing to recover from depression, as well as mental health professionals and activists committed to assisting others in overcoming this crippling affliction. This book is a useful resource that offers practical advice, evidence-based information, and a recovery pathway that can assist individuals in regaining a sense of hope, resilience, and well-being.

Preface

Depression can have a significant influence on a person's quality of life, reducing their ability to work, socialize, and participate in activities they formerly liked. However, it is critical to understand that recovery from depression is possible and that there are evidence-based treatments and strategies available to assist individuals in managing their symptoms and regaining control of their lives.

This book, "Depression Recovery Roadmap," was produced with the intention of giving a thorough path to recovery to people suffering from depression and their loved ones. The book discusses important aspects of depression, such as its causes, symptoms, and evidence-based therapies. It delves into medicine, therapy, lifestyle modifications, coping skills, and the formation of a support network.

The authors of this book have drawn on their significant experience in the mental health sector to present a realistic, sympathetic, and evidence-based road map to recovery. They used simple language and real-life examples to guide readers through the complicated landscape of depression and its treatment alternatives.

It is critical to emphasize that this book is not a replacement for professional assistance. Depression is a serious mental illness that necessitates the knowledge of mental health specialists. This book, on the other hand, can be a useful resource for anyone who wants to understand more about depression and its therapeutic choices. It can also be used as a guide for loved ones who want to help people who are depressed.

We hope that the "Depression Recovery Roadmap" will be a powerful tool for those attempting to recover from depression. We think that with the correct tools and help, people can reclaim control of their lives and feel fresh hope and optimism.

Acknowledgements

Writing a book is a collective endeavor, and we'd like to thank everyone who contributed to making "Depression Recovery Roadmap" a reality.

First and foremost, we would like to express our gratitude to our families and loved ones for their steadfast support during the writing process. Your words of wisdom and understanding have been invaluable.

We'd also like to thank the mental health specialists who shared their knowledge and ideas with us, allowing us to build a thorough guide on depression recovery. We are inspired by your diligent work in the field of mental health.

We'd also like to thank the people who submitted their personal stories on depression. Your bravery and vulnerability have contributed to the creation of a compassionate and informative book.

We would like to express our appreciation to our colleagues who provided criticism, direction, and support during the writing process. Your feedback assisted us in refining our ideas and producing a book that we are glad to offer.

Finally, we'd like to thank our publisher and the many people who contributed to the creation of this book. Your devotion and hard work on this project have helped bring this book to life.

Thank you to everyone who helped with this book in any manner, big or small. We hope that "Depression Recovery Roadmap" will be a useful resource for anyone attempting to recover from depression, and we appreciate your help in making this book a reality.

Introduction

Depression is a frequent and serious mental health problem that affects millions of people around the world. It is often incapacitating, affecting many aspects of a person's life, including their job, relationships, and self-care. While depression can feel overwhelming and isolating, keep in mind that recovery is possible. This book, "Depression Recovery Roadmap," is intended to serve as a resource for those dealing with depression and those who support them.

The purpose of this book is to present a detailed and practical roadmap to depression rehabilitation. It covers the most important aspects of depression, such as its causes, symptoms, and treatment choices. The book delves into a variety of evidence-based therapies, such as medication, counseling, lifestyle modifications, coping skills, and the formation of a support network.

The book is structured into nine chapters, each of which covers a different aspect of depression rehabilitation. The first chapter gives an overview of depression, explaining what it is, what causes it, and how it is diagnosed. The second chapter delves into the symptoms of depression as well as the many types of depression. The third chapter discusses getting professional help for depression and locating a certified mental health expert.

The fourth chapter examines the function of medication in the treatment of depression, including how antidepressant medications operate and their potential negative effects.

Chapter Five delves into many methods of depression therapy, such as cognitive-behavioral therapy and interpersonal therapy. The sixth chapter emphasizes the significance of lifestyle modifications in depression rehabilitation, such as exercise, nutrition, and stress management.

Building a support network, including family, friends, support groups, and internet forums, is covered in Chapter 7. Chapter Eight delves into several coping tactics for depression, such as mindfulness practices and cognitive restructuring. Finally, chapter nine offers advice on staying on the road to recovery, dealing with setbacks, and avoiding relapse.

This book is written in an approachable, easy-to-read format, with straightforward language and practical examples. It is meant to be a useful resource for anyone suffering from depression, their loved ones, and mental health specialists. We hope that this book will serve as a road map to rehabilitation, offering direction and support along the way.

Note: Please keep in mind that this book is only a guide to overcoming depression. If you or someone you know needs a doctor, you or they should go to one. Do not rely solely on this book.

Chapter 1 Depression An Overview

The reader is introduced to the notion of depression in this chapter, including what it is, how it affects individuals, and how it is diagnosed. It describes depression as a significant mental health illness caused by a range of variables such as genetic predisposition, environmental stressors, and chemical imbalances in the brain.

Depression is a mental health condition that affects millions of individuals throughout the world. It is a complex illness with widely varying symptoms, severity, and longevity. Depression can have a substantial impact on a person's capacity to function in everyday life, as well as on relationships, career, and general quality of life.

In this chapter, we will discuss the causes, symptoms, diagnosis, and therapy of depression.

Causes of depression

Depression is a complicated condition with no single identifiable cause. It is usually the result of a mix of genetic, biochemical, environmental, and psychological factors.

According to research, those who have a family history of depression are more likely to develop the condition themselves. Furthermore, some research indicates that certain genetic variations may increase a person's risk of depression.

Certain neurotransmitter imbalances, such as serotonin and dopamine, are biological factors that contribute to depression. These chemicals help control mood and emotions, and when they are out of balance, they can contribute to depression.

Environmental factors can also contribute to depression. Some people experience depression as a result of stressful life events such as the death of a loved one, a job loss, or a significant illness. Chronic stress, such as recurrent financial troubles, interpersonal issues, or job-related stress, can also lead to depression.

A person's risk for depression can also be increased by psychological variables such as negative thought patterns or a history of trauma or abuse.

Symptoms of depression

Depression can appear in a variety of ways, with symptoms varying from person to person. However, some common depression symptoms include:

- Feelings of melancholy, pessimism, or emptiness that persist

- Loss of interest in previously enjoyable activities

- Fatigue or low energy levels

- Sleeping difficulties or excessive sleep

- Appetite or weight changes Difficulty concentrating or making decisions

- Irritability or agitation

- Suicidal or self-harming thoughts

Diagnosis of Depression

Depression can be diagnosed by a mental health professional, such as a psychiatrist or psychologist. Typically, they will perform an assessment that includes a physical examination, a review of the person's medical history, and a discussion of their symptoms.

To be diagnosed with depression, a person must have had persistent feelings of melancholy or a loss of interest in formerly enjoyable activities for at least two weeks. They must also exhibit at least five of the following symptoms: weariness, difficulties sleeping or excessive sleeping, changes in eating or weight, difficulty concentrating or making decisions, irritability or restlessness, and suicidal or self-harming ideas.

Treatment of Depression

Depression is a curable disorder with a range of successful treatment options. Psychotherapy and medication are the most commonly used therapies for depression.

Working with a mental health expert to identify and address the underlying reasons for depression is what psychotherapy, often known as talk therapy, entails. Cognitive-behavioral therapy (CBT) is a popular type of psychotherapy for depression. CBT aims to alter negative thought patterns and behaviors that contribute to depression.

Depression can also be effectively treated with medication. Antidepressant drugs function by modifying the levels of particular neurotransmitters in the brain, such as selective serotonin reuptake inhibitors (SSRIs) and serotonin-norepinephrine reuptake inhibitors (SNRIs).

A combination of psychotherapy and medicine may be the most effective treatment for depression in some circumstances.

Electroconvulsive therapy (ECT) and transcranial magnetic stimulation (TMS) are two other treatments for depression. TMS employs magnetic fields to activate nerve cells in the brain, whereas ECT sends an electrical current across the brain to create a brief seizure.

Depression is a complex mental health illness that can have serious consequences in a person's daily life. While there are numerous causes of depression, there are effective treatment options available, including psychotherapy and medication. If you are suffering from depressive symptoms, it is critical that you seek support from a mental health expert. People suffering from depression can improve their quality of life and recover with the right treatment and support. Raising awareness about depression and reducing the stigma associated with seeking care for mental health issues is critical.

Chapter 2 Symptoms of Depression

This chapter discusses common depression symptoms such as sorrow, irritability, exhaustion, and changes in eating and sleep patterns. It also covers the various kinds of depression, including major depressive disorder, seasonal affective disorder, and postpartum depression. Depression is a widespread mental health condition that affects millions of people worldwide. It is a serious illness that can have a significant impact on a person's life, making it difficult to operate normally and enjoy regular activities. A continuous sense of melancholy, hopelessness, and despair characterizes depression. However, it is critical to recognize that depression is more than just feeling down. It is a complex illness with a wide range of symptoms that can impact several elements of a person's life. This chapter will go over the symptoms of depression in depth.

- **Persistent sadness:**A continuous sense of melancholy is one of the most typical signs of depression. This grief could be unexplainable and unrelated to any specific event or condition. It can linger for several weeks, months, or even years. This continuous sadness can make it difficult to enjoy daily activities and can have an impact on one's overall quality of life.

- **Loss of interest:**Another common symptom of depression is a loss of interest in previously appreciated activities. They may lose interest in hobbies, social activities, jobs, and even time spent with family and friends. This loss of interest can make it difficult to find enjoyment in life and can lead to feelings of isolation and loneliness.

- **Sleep disturbances:**Sleep habits can also be affected by depression. They may have difficulties sleeping or staying asleep, or they may wake up too early. On the other hand, they may sleep excessively and struggle to get out of bed in the morning. These sleep abnormalities can leave a person feeling weary and lethargic, exacerbating their depressive symptoms.

- **Fatigue:**Even after obtaining enough rest, depression can induce a lasting feeling of exhaustion. This weariness can make it difficult to accomplish daily tasks and might result in feelings of exhaustion and weakness.

- **Appetite changes:**Depression can also have an impact on a person's appetite. They may lose their appetite, resulting in weight reduction, or they may overeat, resulting in weight gain. Changes in hunger can have an impact on a person's energy levels and mood.

- **Difficulty concentrating:**Depression can impair one's capacity to concentrate and focus. They may struggle to remember information or make decisions. This might have an impact on their job and personal lives, making it harder for them to complete daily duties.

- **Feelings of guilt or worthlessness:**People suffering from depression frequently experience feelings of guilt or worthlessness. They may believe they are a burden to their loved ones or that they are insufficient. These emotions can be overwhelming, leading to more negative thoughts and behaviors.

- **Thoughts of self-harm or suicide:**In severe circumstances, depression can lead to suicidal or self-harming thoughts. If you or someone you know is having suicidal thoughts or behaviors, you should seek immediate treatment.

Finally, depression is a complicated mental health illness that can have a significant impact on a person's life. If you or someone you know is experiencing these symptoms, it is critical to recognize them and seek treatment. Depression treatment can be beneficial, and with the correct assistance, people suffering from depression can live happy and fulfilled lives.

Chapter 3 Seeking Help for Depression

The significance of obtaining professional therapy for depression is emphasized in this chapter. It describes how to locate a qualified mental health practitioner, what to expect during the initial therapy session, and the numerous depression treatment methods accessible.

Seeking treatment for depression is critical to preventing it from becoming chronic or developing more serious health issues. In this chapter, we'll look at how to get help for depression and the benefits of doing so.

Recognizing Depression

Recognizing the symptoms of depression is the first step in seeking help. Depression can appear in a variety of ways, however, some frequent symptoms include:

- Persistent sadness, anxiety, or emptiness

- Loss of enthusiasm for hobbies or activities

- Fatigue, loss of energy, or feeling constantly exhausted

- Difficulties concentrating, making judgments, or recalling information

- A change in appetite, weight, or sleeping habits

- Irritability, agitation, or restlessness

- Feelings of worthlessness, guilt, or hopelessness

- Suicidal or dying thoughts on a regular basis

If you or someone you know is experiencing these symptoms, you should get medical attention right away. Depression is a treatable disorder, and getting help can make a big difference in your recovery.

Methods for Seeking Assistance

Individual needs and preferences dictate the best way to seek help for depression. Here are a few of the most common:

- **Talk to a Healthcare Professional:**Talking to a healthcare practitioner is the first step in seeking therapy for depression. This can be a family doctor, a psychiatrist, or a psychologist. These specialists can diagnose depression, recommend suitable therapies, and refer patients to other healthcare practitioners if necessary. They may also prescribe and supervise drugs such as antidepressants.

- **Attend Therapy:**Therapy is an effective depression treatment that can assist patients in learning coping skills, identifying triggers, and changing negative thought patterns. Cognitive-behavioral therapy (CBT), interpersonal therapy

(IPT), and psychodynamic therapy are all types of therapy. A therapist can help individuals or groups address specific concerns and build individualized treatment plans.

- **Join a Support Group:**Support groups are gatherings of people who have had similar experiences and can offer emotional support and encouragement. There are support groups for people suffering from depression, where they can connect with others who understand what they're going through. Support groups can be in-person or online, and they can be peer-led or professionally facilitated.

- **Use Self-Help Resources:**self-help options can help people manage their depression symptoms in addition to professional treatment. Books, websites, apps, and podcasts provide information on depression, self-care recommendations, and mindfulness practices.

The Advantages of Seeking Assistance

Seeking assistance for depression can offer a variety of advantages, including:

- Improvements in both mental and physical health

- Better life quality and social functioning

- Relapse risk is reduced.

- Self-awareness and resilience have improved.

- Relationships with family and friends have improved.

It's critical to remember that seeking depression treatment is a sign of strength, not weakness. Depression, like any other sickness, is a medical condition that requires treatment. Seeking support and working with healthcare professionals to establish a personalized treatment plan is the most effective method to overcome depression.

In conclusion, depression is a severe mental illness that can affect anyone, regardless of age, gender, or socioeconomic status. Seeking treatment for depression is critical to preventing it from becoming chronic or developing more serious health issues. Talking to a healthcare practitioner, attending therapy, joining a support group, and using self-help tools are all options for getting aid.

Chapter 4 Medication for Depression

This chapter examines the function of medication in the treatment of depression. It describes how antidepressant medication works, what adverse effects may occur, and how long the medication can take to take action. It also emphasizes the significance of collaborating with a healthcare expert to choose the best drug and dosage.

Depression is a widespread mental illness that affects people of all ages, genders, and socioeconomic situations. It can be caused by a variety of circumstances, including genetic predisposition, environmental stressors, or chemical imbalances in the brain. While psychotherapy is often the first-line treatment for depression, medication can also help manage symptoms and improve overall well-being. In this chapter, we will look at the many types of depression medications, how they work, their potential advantages and side effects, and other things to keep in mind when taking them.

Depression Treatment Options

There are various types of depression medications, each with its own mechanism of action and associated side effects. The following are the most often prescribed classes:

- **Selective Serotonin Reuptake Inhibitors (SSRIs):**SSRIs are antidepressants that function by boosting serotonin levels in the brain, a neurotransmitter that regulates mood. Paxil (Prozac), sertraline (Zoloft), and escitalopram (Lexapro) are examples of SSRIs.

- **SNRIs (Serotonin and Norepinephrine Reuptake Inhibitors):**SNRIs are similar to SSRIs in that they enhance serotonin levels, but they also boost norepinephrine, another neurotransmitter involved in mood regulation. Venlafaxine (Effexor) and duloxetine (Cymbalta) are two examples of SNRIs.

- **Tricyclic antidepressants (TCAs):**TCAs are an older class of antidepressants that function by blocking serotonin and norepinephrine reuptake. Because they have more side effects than newer antidepressants, they are less commonly prescribed today. Amitriptyline (Elavil) and nortriptyline (Pamelor) are two TCAs.

- **Monoamine Oxidase Inhibitors (MAOIs):**MAOIs are another older family of antidepressants that function by reducing the action of monoamine oxidase, an enzyme that breaks down serotonin and norepinephrine. MAOIs are also less routinely administered today due to the risk of harmful interactions with certain foods and drugs. MAOIs such as phenelzine (Nardil) and tranylcypromine (Parnate) are examples.

- **Atypical Antidepressants:**Atypical antidepressants are a class of drugs that do not fit into any of the other categories. They function in a variety of ways, including as blocking specific receptors in the brain or reducing the reuptake of dopamine, another neurotransmitter involved in mood regulation. Bupropion (Wellbutrin) and mirtazapine (Remeron) are two examples of atypical antidepressants.

How Depression Medication Works

Each kind of antidepressant has a different method of action, but they all function by changing the levels of particular neurotransmitters in the brain. Neurotransmitters are chemical messengers that send signals between neurons, and imbalances in neurotransmitter levels are hypothesized to have a role in depression development.

The precise etiology of depression is unknown, but it is assumed to be a complex combination of genetic, environmental, and biochemical variables. An imbalance of several neurotransmitters in the brain, including serotonin, norepinephrine, and dopamine, has been linked to depression as a biological component.

Neurotransmitters are substances that help neurons in the brain communicate with each other. When a signal is sent, a neurotransmitter is released from one neuron into the synapse (the small gap between neurons), where it binds to receptors on the receiving neuron and either triggers or inhibits a signal. The neurotransmitter is then either degraded by enzymes or reabsorbed by the original neuron in a process known as reuptake.

Depression medications act by modifying the amounts of certain neurotransmitters in the brain. Selective serotonin reuptake inhibitors (SSRIs) and serotonin and norepinephrine reuptake inhibitors (SNRIs) are the most often prescribed antidepressant classes.

SSRIs function by inhibiting serotonin reuptake in the synapse, increasing the amount of serotonin available to bind to receptors on the receiving neuron. This can result in increased serotonin signaling, which is known to boost mood and reduce depression symptoms. SNRIs function similarly, but they also inhibit the reuptake of norepinephrine, another neurotransmitter implicated in mood regulation.Other antidepressant classes, such as tricyclic antidepressants (TCAs) and monoamine oxidase inhibitors (MAOIs), function in different ways. TCAs inhibit serotonin and norepinephrine reuptake, but they also inhibit other receptors in the brain, which might result in additional negative effects. MAOIs block the function of a monoamine oxidase enzyme, which breaks down serotonin and norepinephrine. MAOIs boost the amount of these neurotransmitters in the brain by blocking this enzyme, which can improve mood.

Atypical antidepressants are drugs that do not fall cleanly into any of these categories. They function in a variety of ways, including blocking specific receptors in the brain or reducing the reuptake of dopamine, another neurotransmitter involved in mood regulation.

It is crucial to note that the precise mechanism of action of any medicine is unknown and may differ from person to person. Furthermore, because the brain is a complex organ and neurotransmitters are involved in a variety of processes, the relationship between neurotransmitters and depression is still being studied.

Potential Advantages and Drawbacks

Depression medication can be quite useful in reducing symptoms and enhancing the quality of life for people suffering from depression. However, like all medications, they may have side effects.

The following are some of the most prevalent antidepressant adverse effects:

- Nausea

- Dizziness

- Drowsiness

- Insomnia

- gaining weigh

- Sexual dysfunction

These adverse effects can vary based on the medication and the person using it. SSRIs, for example, have fewer adverse effects than TCAs and MAOIs but can still induce sexual dysfunction in certain people.

It's important to note that not everyone will have side effects, and many people find that the advantages of medication outweigh the risks.

Beyond the potential advantages and negative effects of the medicine, there are several more aspects to consider if you are considering taking depression medication.

To begin, it is critical to understand that antidepressant medication is not a cure. While it can be very effective in providing symptom relief, it is not a replacement for therapy or other forms of treatment. In fact, for the best results, most doctors recommend a mix of medicine and therapy.

Second, it is critical to be patient when beginning antidepressant medication. The medication may take several weeks to begin functioning, and it may take many months to get the full therapeutic impact. Side effects are also typical when starting a new medicine, but they usually go away on their own within a few weeks.

Third, when taking depression medication, it is critical to follow your doctor's directions. This includes taking the drug as directed, not discontinuing or modifying the dosage without first visiting your doctor, and reporting any side effects or changes in mood or behavior to your doctor.

Fourth, you should be aware that antidepressant medication can interact with other prescriptions or supplements you may be taking. Before beginning antidepressant medication, inform your doctor of all medications and supplements you are taking.

Finally, you should be aware that antidepressant medication can have an effect on your overall health and well-being. Some medications, for example, may increase the risk of falls or fractures in older adults, or they may interact with other medical conditions you may have. While taking depression medication, it is critical to discuss any concerns you may have with your doctor and to have regular check-ups to monitor your overall health.

In conclusion, medication for depression can be a highly beneficial treatment option for many people, but it's critical to be aware of the potential advantages and side effects, as well as other factors, before making a treatment decision. Working closely with your doctor and being patient and dedicated to your therapy can result in better results.

Chapter 5 Therapy for Depression

This chapter delves into the various types of therapy that can help with depression, such as cognitive-behavioral therapy, interpersonal therapy, and psychodynamic therapy. It also covers the advantages of treatment, such as the development of coping skills, increased self-awareness, and the formation of a support network.

Depression is a widespread mental health condition that affects millions of people worldwide. It is characterized by despair, hopelessness, and worthlessness, and it can disrupt a person's daily life. Fortunately, many effective therapies are available to assist people in managing their symptoms and improving their quality of life. In this chapter, we will look at some of the most common and successful depression treatments.

Cognitive Behavioural Therapy (CBT): One of the most extensively used and investigated treatments for depression is cognitive-behavioral therapy. CBT's major purpose is to assist people in identifying negative thought patterns and replacing them with more positive ones. This therapy can assist individuals in recognizing and challenging negative beliefs that contribute to depression, as well as learning how to replace them with more positive ones. CBT is often delivered through a series of structured sessions with a therapist that includes goal-setting, identifying negative tendencies, and trying to modify them.

Interpersonal Therapy (IPT): Interpersonal therapy is concerned with the enhancement of interpersonal relationships and communication abilities. It can be especially beneficial for people who are depressed as a result of relationship troubles or major life transitions. IPT aims to develop communication and problem-solving skills, as well as help people understand their emotions and how they relate to others. This sort of therapy usually consists of weekly meetings with a therapist and can be done in either individual or group settings.

Psychodynamic Therapy: Psychodynamic treatment is founded on the premise that depression is frequently the result of unresolved past conflicts. This treatment focuses on these conflicts and how they may be influencing current behavior and feelings. Psychodynamic therapy is a longer-term treatment that can take months or even years to finish. It entails investigating the unconscious mind and may employ techniques such as free association and dream analysis to assist individuals in gaining insight into their emotions and behaviors.

Mindfulness-Based Therapies: Mindfulness-based therapies are gaining popularity in the treatment of depression. These therapies teach people how to be more present at the moment and better manage their thoughts and emotions. Mindfulness-based therapies often include guided meditations and mindfulness exercises designed to help people become more aware of their thoughts and feelings. This therapy has been demonstrated to be very useful for patients who have had recurring bouts of depression.

Medication: To treat depression, medication is frequently used in conjunction with treatment. The most commonly prescribed drugs for depression are antidepressants. These drugs operate by raising neurotransmitter levels in the brain, such as serotonin and norepinephrine, which can enhance mood and alleviate depression symptoms. It is critical to remember that medication should only be administered under the supervision of a skilled healthcare expert.

In conclusion, depression may be a crippling disorder that interferes with many parts of a person's life. However, there are numerous effective therapies available to help manage and even overcome depression symptoms. The best therapy will be determined by the individual, their symptoms, and their preferences. Working with a trained mental health practitioner to decide the appropriate course of treatment for each individual's specific requirements is critical.

Chapter 6 Lifestyle Changes for Depression

This chapter emphasizes the significance of lifestyle modifications in depression recovery. It looks at how exercise, nutrition, sleep, and stress management can help improve mental health and well-being. It also includes helpful hints for implementing these adjustments and incorporating them into daily life.

Depression is a severe mental illness that affects millions of people worldwide. While therapy and medication are frequently required for the treatment of depression, certain lifestyle changes can also help manage the condition. Here are some lifestyle changes that can help with depression treatment.

- **Exercise regularly:**Regular physical activity has been demonstrated to improve mood and minimize symptoms of depression. Endorphins, which are natural compounds that boost mood and lessen pain, are released during exercise. It also increases the formation of new brain cells, which can aid in the improvement of cognitive function.

- **Get enough sleep:**Sleep is essential for overall health, and a lack of sleep might raise the risk of depression. Adults should sleep seven to nine hours per night, while children and teenagers require more. Setting a regular sleep pattern and practicing excellent sleep hygiene will help you get adequate restful sleep.

- **Eat a healthy diet:**A balanced diet can assist to boost mood and lessen depression symptoms. A diet rich in fruits, vegetables, whole grains, lean proteins, and healthy fats can supply your body with the resources it requires to function properly. It is also crucial to avoid processed foods, sugary drinks, and excessive amounts of coffee and alcohol.

- **Use relaxation techniques:**relaxation practices such as meditation, deep breathing, and yoga can help reduce tension and anxiety, two factors that are frequently related to depression. These strategies can also help lift one's mood and boost one's sense of well-being.

- **Create a helpful social network:**Creating a supportive social network can aid in the reduction of feelings of isolation and loneliness, which can lead to depression. Spending time with friends and family, joining a support group, and volunteering can all contribute to a sense of belonging and community.

- **Reduce stress:**Stress can contribute to the onset and worsening of depression. Finding strategies to relieve stress, such as using relaxation techniques or engaging in fun activities, can help boost mood and reduce depression symptoms.

Finally, making certain lifestyle changes can help with depression management. These modifications include regular exercise, adequate sleep, a good diet, relaxation techniques, the development of a supportive social network, and stress reduction. While these changes will not cure depression on their own, they will help to improve mood and overall well-being. It is critical to remember that depression is a serious disorder that requires professional attention from a mental health expert for effective treatment.

Chapter 7 Building a Support Network

This chapter highlights the significance of establishing a support network in the recovery process from depression. It delves into the various sorts of assistance accessible, such as family, friends, support groups, and internet communities. It also explains how to create and manage a support network.

Creating a Support System: There are numerous obstacles in life that can be overwhelming to navigate on our own. This is where having a support network might come in handy. A support network is a collection of people who offer emotional, practical, and even financial assistance when we are in need. Creating a support network can be beneficial to our mental and physical health, personal development, and overall enjoyment.

Finding Potential Support Groups: The first stage in creating a support network is identifying potential sources of assistance. Family members, friends, coworkers, neighbors, community organizations, and professional services are all examples of this. Consider people with whom you are comfortable and who have a positive influence on your life. It is also critical to determine the type of assistance you require. Do you require emotional support, practical help, or advice? Different types of support may be better suited to different people.

Relationship Development: Once you've identified potential sources of assistance, it's critical to nurture these relationships. This entails devoting time and effort to developing and sustaining meaningful relationships with those in your support network. Spending quality time together, staying in touch on a regular basis, and expressing real interest in their lives are all examples of this. It's critical to remember that creating a support network is a two-way street, and it's equally crucial to be there for people.

Communicating Your Requirements: Communicating your requirements is one of the most critical components of developing a support network. It's fine to ask for assistance when you need it, but it's also vital to be explicit about what you require and how others may assist you. Because people in your support network may not always understand what you're going through, it's critical that you communicate openly and honestly. This can be difficult, especially if you're used to dealing with situations on your own, but it's an important component of developing a strong support network.

Being Dependable and Reliable: Being reliable and dependable is another crucial part of developing a support network. This includes being there for others when they need help, as well as keeping promises and showing up when you say you will. Being dependable fosters trust in your connections, which is critical for sustaining a strong support network.

Seeking Professional Assistance: While friends and family can be a great source of support, there may be times when professional assistance is required. Seeking out a therapist, counselor, or other mental health expert is one option. These experts can offer specialized assistance and guidance, and they can be a vital part of your support network.

Finally, developing a support network is critical to our personal and emotional well-being. It can assist us in navigating life's challenges, developing resilience, and promoting happiness and fulfillment. We may develop a robust support network that will serve us well throughout our lives by identifying potential sources of support, nurturing relationships, articulating our requirements, being reliable and dependable, and getting professional help when necessary.

Chapter 8 Coping Strategies for Depression

This chapter looks at several coping mechanisms for dealing with depression. It goes over mindfulness practices, relaxation exercises, and cognitive restructuring. It also includes helpful hints for dealing with negative thoughts and emotions, reducing stress, and boosting self-care.

Coping with depression can be difficult, and it's critical to develop appropriate coping methods to control symptoms and enhance your overall well-being. In this chapter, we'll look at some of the most successful depression coping tactics.

Seek Professional Assistance: Seeking professional therapy is the first and most crucial step in dealing with depression. A mental health specialist can assist you in understanding your symptoms, making an accurate diagnosis, and providing personalized treatment options. Your healthcare professional may recommend psychotherapy, medicine, or a mix of the two based on your specific needs.

Create a Support System: A supportive network of friends and family can assist you in coping with depression. Make an effort to contact and spend time with loved ones on a regular basis. If you don't have a tight support system, consider joining a support group or reaching out to an online depression community.

Practice Self-Care: When dealing with depression, it is critical to take care of yourself. Make an effort to consume a nutritious diet, exercise regularly, and sleep well. Alcohol and narcotics should be avoided because they might aggravate depression symptoms. Participate in activities you enjoy, such as reading, performing music, or spending time in nature.

Learn to Deal with Stress: Stress can exacerbate depression symptoms, therefore it's critical to learn how to manage stress efficiently. Consider deep breathing, meditation, or yoga as relaxation strategies. Make time for relaxing activities such as taking a warm bath or getting a massage.

Negative Thoughts Must Be Challenged: Negative ideas can contribute to depression, so learning how to challenge them is essential. When you detect negative ideas, consider whether they are grounded in reality. Consider whether there is evidence to support them or whether they are founded on false assumptions or ideas. Reframe negative thoughts to make them more positive.

Set attainable objectives: Setting realistic objectives might help you feel accomplished and boost your self-esteem. Make a list of goals that are attainable and work towards them one step at a time. Celebrate your accomplishments, no matter how minor they may appear.

Maintain a Journal: Journaling can be an effective approach to processing your ideas and emotions. Consider keeping a notebook in which you can record your feelings and thoughts. You can also keep a notebook to track your progress toward your goals and to keep track of any tactics that have helped you manage your depression symptoms.

To summarize, managing depression can be difficult, but there are numerous ways that can help you manage your symptoms and improve your overall well-being. Remember to seek professional assistance, create a support system, practice self-care, learn stress management, fight negative beliefs, set realistic objectives, and keep a journal. You can build effective coping skills that work for you with time and effort.

Chapter 9 Staying on the Path to Recovery

This final chapter offers advice on how to stay on the road to recovery. It looks at how to deal with setbacks and avoid relapse, such as sticking to good habits, being connected to a support network, and continuing therapy and medication as needed. It also emphasizes the value of self-compassion and applauds one's progress in the rehabilitation process.

Recovering from depression involves commitment, perseverance, and patience. While there may be ups and downs along the way, it's critical to stay on track and make progress toward your goals. In this chapter, we'll look at several ways to stay on the road to recovery from depression.

Follow Your Treatment Plan: It is critical to follow your treatment plan if you are receiving treatment for depression. This could include taking medicine, going to treatment, or both. It is critical to carefully follow your healthcare provider's recommendations and take your medications as directed. Before making any modifications to your treatment plan, discuss them with your healthcare provider.

Keep an eye on your symptoms: It is critical to check your progress and notice any changes in your symptoms on a frequent basis. Keep a journal or use a symptom monitoring app to keep track of any changes in your mood, energy levels, or sleep patterns. If you detect any substantial changes, contact your healthcare practitioner right away.

Exercise mindfulness: Mindfulness is a strategy that involves focusing on the present moment without judgment. It can help you reduce tension and anxiety while also improving your general well-being. Consider meditating, deep breathing, or using other relaxation techniques to practice awareness.

Take care of yourself: Recovering from depression is a time-consuming and labor-intensive process. It is critical to be gentle with yourself and to practice self-compassion. Don't berate yourself if you experience a setback or a bad day. Instead, concentrate on how you can get back on track and move forward.

To summarize, staying on the road to recovery from depression takes commitment, endurance, and patience. Remember to follow your treatment plan, monitor your for symptoms, practice self-care, create a support system, set reasonable objectives, practice mindfulness, and be gentle with yourself. You can continue to make progress toward your recovery and enhance your general well-being with time and effort.

Chapter 10 Conclusion

In conclusion, "Depression Recovery Roadmap" is a thorough manual that attempts to give a route to recovery for people suffering from depression and their loved ones. The book delves into key themes about depression, such as its causes, symptoms, and treatment methods. It emphasizes the necessity of seeking professional help, forming a support network, changing one's lifestyle, and developing coping techniques to deal with depression.

This book provides readers with practical counsel in the form of plain language and real-life experiences to help them navigate their route to recovery from depression. It emphasizes the need for self-compassion and recognizes the progress made on the road to recovery. The book emphasizes that depression recovery is achievable, and that, with the correct tools and assistance, people can take control of their lives and enjoy a renewed sense of hope and optimism.

Finally, "Depression Recovery Roadmap" is a great resource for everyone wishing to recover from depression, especially those suffering from it and their loved ones. It presents a step-by-step guide to rehabilitation and emphasizes the need for seeking professional help, establishing a support network, and developing coping strategies. The book will be a powerful tool for people who want to take charge of their mental health and live fulfilled lives.

www.ingramcontent.com/pod-product-compliance
Lightning Source LLC
Chambersburg PA
CBHW070612160726
48003CB00005B/2227